LIBRARY

Polly and the Frog and other folk tales

What happened when Polly kept her promise? How did the shepherd win the heart of a princess? And why did the parrot save the hunter?

Find out in this delightful collection of folk tales from around the world. These imaginative retellings bring the stories vividly to life and are full of action and fun.

ᵻ Hartman is a widely acclaimed ᵤr and storyteller. He is best known for *The Lion Storyteller Bible* and other books in the *Storyteller* series in which these tales were originally published.

Medway Libraries

C050822952

Polly and the Frog

and other folk tales

Bob Hartman

Illustrations by
Brett Hudson

LION
Children's Books

Medway Library & Information Service	
C050822952	
Peters	
	£3.99

Text copyright © 1998 and 2002 Bob Hartman
Illustrations copyright © 2004 Brett Hudson of GCI
This edition copyright © 2004 Lion Hudson

The moral rights of the author and illustrator
have been asserted

A Lion Children's Book
an imprint of
Lion Hudson plc
Mayfield House, 256 Banbury Road,
Oxford OX2 7DH, England
www.lionhudson.com
ISBN 0 7459 4698 4

First edition 2004
10 9 8 7 6 5 4 3 2 1 0

All rights reserved

Acknowledgments
These stories were first published in *The Lion
Storyteller Bedtime Book* and *The Lion Storyteller
Book of Animal Tales*

A catalogue record for this book is available
from the British Library

Typeset in 15/23 Baskerville MT Schlbk
Printed and bound in Great Britain
by Cox and Wyman Ltd, Reading

Contents

The Shepherd and the Clever Princess

Princess Vendla could speak any language.
Any language in the world!

German, French.

Italian, Polish.

Chinese, Zulu, English.

She could understand them all.

Her father, the king, was proud of her. So proud, in fact, that he set a challenge for all the young men in his kingdom.

'If you want to marry my daughter,' he announced, 'you must first speak to her in a language she does not understand. Succeed, and she shall be your bride. Fail, and you shall be thrown into the sea!'

Many men tried. Wise men. Rich men. Handsome men. But, sadly, each and every one of them ended up in the sea.

And then, one day, Timo the shepherd boy decided that it was time to find a wife.

'They say the princess is quite pretty,' he said to himself. 'So I shall take up the king's challenge and make her my bride.'

Now Timo was neither wise, nor rich, nor handsome. In fact, he was a dreamer, who wandered through the forests and across the fields chatting with the birds and whispering to the animals.

Timo set off for the king's palace. He
hadn't gone far when he heard a noise – a
chippery, chirping noise – the cry of a little
bird. But the noise wasn't falling down from
somewhere high in the trees. No, it was
leaping up from somewhere on the ground.

Timo followed the noise. He brushed
away branches and bark and old, dead
leaves. And soon he found it – a sad young
sparrow with a badly broken wing.

'Poor little fellow,' Timo said. 'You're lucky you haven't been gobbled up by a fox or a cat. Why don't you ride with me for a while?'

And Timo picked up the little sparrow and set him gently in his big leather pouch.

Timo walked a little further and soon he heard another noise – a scritchity, scratching noise that could come only from a squirrel.

'I'm caught. I'm caught in a trap!' the little squirrel chattered. 'Won't somebody please help me?'

Timo was there in a minute. He loosened the sharp wire from around the squirrel's leg. Then he picked him up and put him in his pouch next to the sparrow.

'You can rest there,' he whispered to the squirrel, 'until your leg is better.'

Timo started off for the king's palace, once again, but it wasn't long before he heard yet another noise – a crawing, caw-cawing noise, high above his head.

'What's the matter, Mr Crow?' Timo called.

'I have lost my wife!' cawed the crow. 'The king's hunters were out in the woods, and I fear they have taken her. I have been flying in circles for hours and I cannot find her.'

'Why not come with me?' said Timo.
'I am going to the king's palace this very
day. You can hop into my pouch and ride
along.'

The tired crow gladly accepted Timo's
offer, and before long, the shepherd boy
and his secret companions were at the
palace gates.

'Who goes there?' shouted the watchman.

'It's Timo, the shepherd boy. I have come
to marry the princess.'

'You mean you've come to be tossed into
the sea!' the watchman laughed. 'Men wiser
and richer than yourself have found their
way there already.'

'Perhaps,' Timo nodded. 'But they did
not know what I know – a language that
Princess Vendla will not understand.'

The watchman let Timo into the palace,
and then led him to the king.

'Your Majesty,' Timo bowed, 'I have
come to take up your challenge. I believe
I know a language that your daughter will
not understand.'

The king could not keep himself from
laughing.

'But you are just a poor shepherd boy,'
he chuckled. 'And my daughter has studied
every language in the world! The sea is very

cold at this time of year. Are you sure you want to accept my challenge?'

'I do,' Timo nodded. 'I want to see the princess.'

The king called for his daughter, and she was the most beautiful girl young Timo had ever seen. He bowed to the princess, then he reached his hand into his leather pouch and gently scratched the little sparrow's head.

'Chip-chirp-chippery-chirp,' said the sparrow.

Timo looked at Princess Vendla. 'Can you tell me what that means?' he asked.

Princess Vendla looked very worried. 'Why, no,' she said slowly, 'I can't.'

'It means: "Thank you for rescuing me, Timo. My wing is much better now."'

Timo reached his hand into his pouch

again, and this time he tickled the squirrel under his furry chin.

'Scrick-scrack-scrickity-scrack,' said the squirrel. And again the princess could only shake her head.

'This is an easy one,' said Timo. 'It means: "Thank you for the ride and for saving me from the hunter's trap.'"

Timo reached his hand once more
into his pouch, but before he could nudge
the crow, the king stood up and shouted,
'Enough! I am ashamed of you, Daughter.
I gave you the finest teachers in the world
and yet this ignorant shepherd boy knows
more than you!'

'I'm sorry, Father,' the princess sobbed,
'perhaps I am not as clever as you thought.'

'Oh no, Princess,' said Timo. 'You are
very clever indeed. Clever enough to admit
that there are things you still must learn.
That is the beginning of real wisdom, and
I admire you all the more for it.'

The king smiled when he heard these
words. He announced that Timo and
Vendla should be married that very day,

and everyone in the palace cheered.

So it was that Timo came to live at the
palace. And, with the help of the sparrow,
the squirrel, the crows, and all his other
woodland friends, he taught Princess Vendla
the language of the animals.

And they all lived happily ever after.

The Boastful Toad

Bull was big. Bull was bulky. Bull was
brawny and bulgy and brown.

But despite his size (or, perhaps, because
of it!), Bull was no bully. He was gentle and
quiet and bothered no one.

Toad, on the other hand, was tiny. Tinier
than Pig, tinier than Dog, tinier than Cat.
And much, much tinier than Bull.

But despite his size (or, perhaps, because

of it!), he never stopped saying how
wonderful he was.

'I can jump much higher than you!' he
boasted to Pig, who could not jump very
high at all.

'That may be true,' Pig grunted, 'but
there's no need to point it out to me.'

'I can kill more flies than you!' he boasted
to Dog, who had never eaten an insect in
his life.

'That may be true,' woofed Dog, 'but
nobody likes a show-off.'

'I can swim much
further than you!'
he boasted to
Cat, who hated
even getting her
paws wet.

'That may be true,' Cat miaowed, 'but you'd better be careful, Toad. Your boasting is going to get you into trouble some day!'

And then, one bright morning, Toad decided to boast to Bull.

Bull was in his field, chewing on a thick patch of weeds, when Toad hopped right up beside him.

Toad looked up at Bull, all big and brown and bulky. And he thought hard about his very best boasts.

Bull could jump higher than Toad, there was no doubt about that. Toad had seen him kill hundreds of flies with his tail. And as for swimming, Toad had watched Bull paddle right across the river! So none of those boasts was going to work.

And then he remembered something –

a clever trick an old toad had taught him when he was hardly more than a tadpole.

'I can make myself bigger than you!' he shouted at Bull. And Bull nearly choked on his mouthful of weeds.

'That may well be true,' said Bull, 'but I'm going to have to see it to believe it.'

So Toad looked Bull right in the eye. Then he stood up on his tippy toes and

sucked in a big breath of air. And sure enough, he blew himself up to twice his size!

'That's an amazing trick,' Bull nodded. But it was plain to both of them that Toad was still nowhere near as big as Bull.

'I can get bigger still!' Toad boasted. And he sucked in an even bigger breath of air.

'Now be careful there, little fellow,' warned Bull. But Toad was determined to prove that he was right. And he blew himself up to four times his size!

But he was still much smaller than Bull. So he started to suck in another big breath of air.

'I think you should stop right there,' said Bull.

But Toad kept on sucking in air.

'It's not important how big you are,' Bull

snorted. 'It really isn't!'

But Toad still kept on sucking in air.

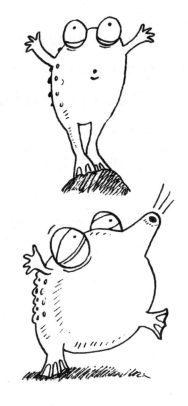

'All right. You can make yourself bigger than me. I believe it,' said Bull. 'Just stop. Please!'

But it was plain to Toad that he was still not big enough. Not yet. So he shut his eyes and concentrated and sucked in one more breath of air…

All the other animals heard

a 'bang' somewhere off in the fields. And when they went to investigate, Bull was standing there, shaking his big brown head.

'I told him to be careful,' Bull sighed. 'I warned him.'

'I know,' miaowed Cat. 'I told him that his boasting would get him into trouble one day.'

And so it had. For with all his boasting and puffing himself up, poor Toad had blown himself into a million tiny pieces.

Polly and the Frog

Polly had a very wicked stepmother. Her own mother had died when Polly was just a little girl. And the woman her father had married did not like Polly. Not one little bit. So she made Polly do the hardest jobs around the house. And if Polly did not do them perfectly, she was punished. As for Polly's father, he loved the woman so much that he would do nothing to stop her.

One day, the wicked stepmother called
for Polly. And, very sternly, she said, 'Girl,'
(for she never called Polly by name) 'take
this sieve to the well, fill it with water, and
bring it straight back to me.'

Polly knew this was impossible! For the
sieve was full of holes and she could never
fill it with water. No one could!

Polly said nothing. She just nodded her

head and walked slowly to the well. But when she got there, all she could do was plonk herself down at the side of the well and weep.

'Bar-durp,' came a voice from inside the well. 'Bar-durp. Bar-durp.'

Polly wiped her eyes on her sleeve and looked down into the well.

And there was a frog – the biggest, fattest, friendliest frog she had ever seen.

'Bar-durp,' said the frog again. 'You don't look very happy, young lady. Can you tell me what's the matter?'

'It's my stepmother,' Polly sniffled, forgetting all those warnings about never talking to strange frogs. 'She wants me to fill this sieve with water. It's impossible, I know, but if I don't do it she'll punish me the minute I get home.'

'It's not impossible at all!' the frog bar-durped. 'I'll tell you how to do it, if you'll promise me one thing.'

'Anything!' Polly sobbed.

'You must do everything I ask of you for one whole night! Bar-durp.'

Well, it seemed a strange thing to ask, but Polly was desperate. And besides, this frog didn't even know where she lived.

'All right,' Polly agreed. 'Now tell me, please.'

'Bar-durp. Take some moss and some old leaves and jam them into the holes. Then the water won't leak out.'

Polly did what the frog suggested and, sure enough, it worked!

'Thank you!' she smiled. 'You've saved my life!'

'Bar-durp,' the frog smiled back. 'Just remember your promise.' And he did a fat bellyflop back into the water.

Polly hurried home, and her stepmother was so amazed that, for once, she didn't even try to find something wrong with Polly's work. But, later that night, as Polly was finishing her dinner, there was a knock at the door.

'Polly,' her father called. 'There's a frog here to see you.'

Polly swallowed the mouthful of food she was chewing, then rose slowly and walked to the front door. The fat, friendly frog was dripping all over the front mat.

'So it's Polly, is it?' croaked the frog. 'Nice name. Do you mind if I – bar-durp – come in?'

Polly minded very much. But she also remembered her promise. So she invited him in, and then added, very quickly, 'But we're in the middle of dinner.'

'Oh that's all right,' the frog said, flicking out his fat tongue, 'I could do with a snack, myself. Bar-durp.'

Polly returned to the dining room with the frog hopping happily behind her. At first, her stepmother looked angry, and then a wicked smile slithered across her face. This

was the perfect opportunity to make fun of
her pretty stepdaughter.

'Oh, I sec you've found a new friend!' she
sneered. 'He seems a perfect match for you.'

'Bar-durp,' said the frog. 'It's very hard to
see down here. Could I hop onto your lap?'

What could Polly do? She had promised.
So she picked the frog up (he was very slimy!)
and put him on her lap.

The stepmother laughed. She giggled. She guffawed. This was very funny indeed.

Then the frog made his next request.

'Your food smells very good. Bar-durp. Do you think I could have a bite?'

The stepmother was howling now. 'Yes, yes!' she laughed. 'Let's see you feed your little froggy friend!'

Polly sighed and shook her head. Then she scooped up a bit of her dinner and fed it to the frog.

'MMMM,' said the frog. 'Delicious. Bar-durp.'

'Perhaps the froggy would like a drink, as well,' the stepmother teased.

'No, thank you,' the frog croaked. 'But I do have one more request. I wonder if Polly would kiss me – right here on the cheek!'

The stepmother coughed, then choked, then shrieked with laughter.

Polly turned bright red.

'I thought you were my friend,' she whispered to the frog.

'I am. Bar-durp. Trust me – friends keep their promises.'

'So they do,' sighed Polly. And she shut her eyes and kissed the frog on his green, slimy cheek...

But when Polly opened her eyes, the frog was gone! And in his place sat the most handsome young man she had ever seen!

'You've done it!' he shouted, leaping off her lap and dancing for joy. 'You've broken the curse and now I'm free again! Will you come with me to my castle tonight and be my princess?'

Polly looked at her father and her

stepmother. Her father looked amazed
and the wicked stepmother was no longer
laughing.

'Yes,' she said at last. 'Yes, I will. I think
I would like that very much. But what about
them?'

'Well,' said the prince, as he stared at the
stepmother, 'we do have a great many wells
and a kitchen full of sieves. I suppose we
could used the help.'

'No, please don't worry,' the stepmother
muttered. 'We'll stay right here.'

'Yes,' her father agreed. 'You two young
people go off and enjoy yourselves.'

And so they did. Polly married the prince.
They went to live in his castle. And the girl
who kept her promise to a fat, friendly frog
lived happily after after. Bar-durp.

The Kind Parrot

Hunter went into the jungle to hunt. He hunted for rabbits. He hunted for squirrels. He hunted for deer and monkeys and wild pigs. But every time he raised his bow, his prey jumped or ducked or scurried out of sight.

Hunter was hungry. Hunter was tired. And then Hunter saw a parrot, bright yellow and blue, in the branches of a tree. So

Hunter raised his
bow. And Hunter
aimed straight
and true. But as
he went to release the
arrow, Hunter heard the parrot singing
a little song:

Hunter be good. Hunter be kind.
Spare my life and you will find
A reward, a promise, sure and true.
Goodness and kindness will return to you.

Hunter dropped the arrow. Hunter lowered
his bow. And as he did, the parrot flew
away, bright yellow and blue, into the
jungle.

And that's when Hunter heard a sound.
Something was running through the jungle –

running right at him through the bushes and the trees. It could have been a panther, a hyena or a wolf. He could not tell. He could not see. So, afraid, he let an arrow fly. But when he went to see what he had killed, he realized that it was not an animal at all. No, it was the brother of one of the most important men in his village!

Hunter was heartbroken. He carried the man's body back to the village. He tried to explain what had happened. He told the village elders that it was an accident. But no one believed him. And so they sentenced him to die!

On that very day, however, the village was visited by the king. Hunter's wife went to the king. She explained what had happened. She begged him to save Hunter's life.

The king listened carefully to her story.
And then he gave her his decision.

'I will give your husband one chance to
save himself,' the king said. 'A test, to see if
he is telling the truth. Tonight, we will have
a party in the village to celebrate my visit.
We will all be dressed in costumes. If your
husband can pick me out of the crowd, then
his life will be spared.'

The woman hardly knew what to say.

Her husband had a chance – yes. But how
would he ever pick out the king?

As soon as the party had begun, the
guards were told to bring Hunter to
the middle of the village. Just as the king
had said, everyone was dressed in costume.
Some looked like animals. Some looked like
clowns. And Hunter's wife wept when she
saw that many were dressed like kings!

She looked at her husband, but Hunter just sighed. Try as he might, he could not spot the king. He lifted his eyes to heaven, to pray for help. And just at that moment, Hunter saw something else – a flash of colour, bright yellow and blue, in the branches above his head. And then he heard a song, in a voice that he recognized at once:

Hunter be good. Hunter be kind.
You spared my life and now you will find
A king wearing rags, nothing shiny or new.
Goodness and kindness will return to you.

Hunter peered into the crowd, and, sure enough, there among all the fancy costumes stood someone dressed as a beggar.

'That's him!' cried Hunter. 'That's the

king! The one dressed in rags!'

And as soon as he'd said it, the crowd erupted in laughter.

'Ridiculous!' sniggered one of the guards.

'He's finished!' snorted another.

But when the beggar removed his rags and took off his mask, it was indeed the king.

'Set him free!' the king commanded. 'A man wise enough to see a king through a beggar's robes must surely be telling the truth!'

And so Hunter's life was spared. He joined in the party, of course – he had more to celebrate than anyone there. And as he walked home with his wife, he caught sight, one last time, of the parrot, bright yellow and blue. And he heard the bird sing one last time:

Hunter be good. Hunter be kind.
Remember this day and you will find
That you spared my life, I saved yours too!
Goodness and kindness have returned to you.

The Amazing Pine Cone

When the old man wandered into town, no
one paid attention. He tipped his tattered
cap. He waved his wrinkled hand. But
everyone ignored him, for he looked just
like a beggar.

When the old man wandered through
town, he tottered up the hill to the mayor's
house. The house was big and bright and
beautiful. It was the finest house in town by

far. The old man raised his gnarled cane and rapped on the front door.

'What do you want?' called the mayor's wife, as she eased the door open and peered through the gap.

'A place to stay,' the man replied, 'to rest for just one night.'

The mayor's wife looked at the old man. She looked at his tattered cap. She looked at his shabby coat. And she quickly shut the door.

'Go away!' she shouted. 'We have no room for beggars here!'

The old man wandered back through town. He tipped his tattered cap. He waved his wrinkled hand. And still no one paid any attention. He came, at last, to another house – a poor, pathetic, little place. And he rapped on the door with his cane.

A poor, little woman answered the door. And when she saw the old man and his beggar's clothes, she felt sorry for him.

'How can I help you?' she asked.

'I need a place to stay,' said the old man again, 'to rest for just one night.'

'Of course!' she smiled. And she welcomed him into her home.

Next morning, the old man rose early, but before he said goodbye, he reached into his pocket with his wrinkled hand.

'I want to give you something,' he said to the woman. 'It is my way of saying thank you.'

And he handed the woman a pine cone!

The woman didn't know what to say. No one had ever given her a pine cone before.

So she smiled as politely as she could, and tried very hard not to giggle.

'This is no ordinary pine cone,' the old man explained. 'It is a magic pine cone. And it will multiply by a thousand times the first thing you do today!'

The woman smiled again. She liked the old man. She appreciated his kindness. But this was the strangest thing she had ever heard.

She said goodbye, and when the old man

had gone, she turned to a piece of cloth she had woven the night before. She pulled it out of the basket to fold it, but the more she pulled out and the more she folded, the more cloth there was! Soon, not only her living room, but her kitchen and her bedroom and the whole of the house was filled with brand new cloth.

The woman shook her head, amazed. So it really was a magic pine cone after all! And it wasn't long before the whole town learned of the woman's good fortune and the old man's magical gift.

Exactly one year later, the old man wandered into the town again. This time no one ignored him. He tipped his tattered cap. He waved his wrinkled hand. And everyone stopped and smiled and invited him to spend the night.

But, just as he had done before, he wandered through the town to the top of the hill, and knocked on the mayor's door.

The mayor's wife welcomed him with open arms. She gave him the nicest room and the most comfortable bed, and she cooked him a delicious meal.

And as soon as he had gone to bed, she put a pile of gold coins on the table, ready to be counted the moment she received his thank you gift.

Next morning, just as she had expected, the old man reached into his pocket and handed her a pine cone.

'This is no ordinary pine cone,' he explained. 'It is a magic pine cone. And it will multiply by a thousand times the first thing you do today.'

The mayor's wife nodded and smiled. She could hardly wait for the old man to go. And, as soon as she had shut the door behind him, she raced to the table, ready to count her gold. But before she got there, something happened. Something she had not expected.

The mayor's wife sneezed. And because
that was the first thing she did, she sneezed
not once, not twice, but a thousand times –
for the rest of that day, and the next, and
the one after that!

The whole town heard of it, of course.
News even reached the old man, who
smiled and patted his pocketful of pine
cones, and then wandered off to another
town, tipping his tattered cap, waving his
wrinkled hand, and looking for somewhere
to spend the night.

The Dog and the Wolf

One moonlit night, Wolf went out hunting.
Hours passed, and he had nothing to show
for all his hard work. He was hungry and
he was tired, so he sneaked into Farmer's
yard, in the hope of finding a stray duck
or chicken. But all he found was Dog!

Dog growled and bared his teeth. But
before he could raise the alarm, Wolf crept
over to him and whispered, 'Brother Dog,

keep quiet, I beg you. I have not come to steal. No, I simply wanted to ask about your health. It has been so long since we've talked.'

Dog could not remember ever having spoken to Wolf before. But he did seem genuinely interested in having a conversation. And it did get lonely out in the yard at night. So Dog stopped his growling and began, instead, to talk.

'I'm very well, actually,' he said. 'Thank you for asking.' And not wanting to be rude, he asked in return, 'How are you?'

Wolf glanced around the farmyard – not a chicken in sight!

'Ah well, I've had better days,' he confessed.

'I can see that,' Dog admitted. 'You look like you haven't eaten for ages!' (Dog had a

lot to learn about tact!) 'As for me, well, as
you can plainly see, I get plenty to eat.
Dog food, twice a day – and scraps from
Farmer's table!'

'Really?' said Wolf, suddenly just a little
jealous. 'I had no idea.'

'There's more!' Dog went on (he was
enjoying this conversation!). 'When I'm tired,
I don't have to find some hard spot on the

ground to sleep. No, I can curl up in my own little house, here!'

'A house of your own!' nodded Wolf. 'Very nice.' And he thought about the night before, when he'd tried to sleep, wet and shivering, in the rain.

'And if it gets too cold,' Dog continued, 'Farmer will often let me sleep inside, right in front of the fireplace!'

'Oooh!' sighed Wolf. 'I bet that's cosy!' Now he had forgotten all about chickens and ducks. He just wanted to hear more about Dog. And Dog was happy to oblige.

'Where do I start?' he said. 'Playing "catch" in the fields. Doggie treats at Christmas. And do you see this shiny coat of mine? Farmer's wife combs it and brushes it and pulls out every burr and twig.'

Wolf was impressed. So impressed, in fact, that he couldn't help blurting out, 'I wish I was a dog!'

'Well, why not?' said Dog. 'We need someone to watch the other side of the yard. And you've got what it takes – sharp teeth, a keen sense of smell, plus you know all the prowlers' tricks!'

'Let's go!' cried Wolf. 'Let's talk to Farmer now!'

But Dog grew suddenly quiet.

'We'd best wait till morning,' he said. 'Farmer doesn't like to be wakened. And, besides, there's the small matter of this chain.'

Wolf looked closely, and, yes, there was indeed a chain attached, at one end, to a post in the ground. And fastened, at the

other end, to something round Dog's neck.

'And what's that?' asked Wolf, pointing
to the collar.

'That?' Dog shrugged. 'That's just
Farmer's way of saying that he owns me.'

'Owns you?' asked Wolf. And as he said
it, he started to creep slowly away.

'What's the matter?' asked Dog. 'Don't
you want to live here any more?'

'No thank you,' said Wolf. 'A full belly, a warm fireplace and a roof over my head sound very nice indeed. But they are not worth the price of my freedom!'

Then Wolf turned and ran off into the moonlit night – hungry, yes, but free.

The Mole's Bridegroom

The Mole Lord had a lovely mole daughter.
When the time came for her to marry, he
decided that she should wed nothing less
than the greatest thing in all the world. So
he called together the wisest moles in Japan
to help him find her a husband.

The moles scratched their thin mole
beards and squinted their weak mole
eyes. They thought very hard. And, at

last, one mole stood and spoke.

'Surely, the greatest thing in all the world,' he said, 'is the sun.'

'That's the answer then!' exclaimed the Mole Lord. 'My daughter shall marry the sun!'

'Wait just a minute,' said another mole, rising to his pale mole feet. 'The sun may be

great. But, all around the sun, we see the sky. So, surely, that is the greatest thing in all the world.'

'So be it!' declared the Mole Lord. 'My daughter shall marry the sky!'

'Not so fast,' said yet another mole, tapping his long mole nose. 'The sky is sometimes covered by clouds. So, surely, a cloud is the greatest thing in all the world.'

'Excellent!' shouted the Mole Lord. 'My daughter shall marry a cloud!'

'Wait!' sighed another mole, scratching his smooth mole head. 'Am I not right in saying that a strong wind can blow away any cloud? So, surely, the wind must be the greatest thing in all the world!'

'Brilliant!' grinned the Mole Lord. 'My daughter shall marry the wind!'

'But no matter how hard the wind blows,' suggested yet another mole, 'it cannot move the earth! So, surely, the earth is the greatest thing in all the world!'

'Then it's settled,' declared the Mole Lord. 'My daughter shall marry the earth!'

'Yes, yes, yes,' muttered the oldest, greyest and wisest mole of them all. 'The earth may be hard. The earth may be strong. But what can dig a hole in the earth? A mole – that's what! And so I say, surely, a mole is the greatest thing in all the world.'

'Why didn't I think of that?' asked the Mole Lord. 'It's so obvious!'

And that is how the daughter of the Mole Lord came to marry… a mole!

A Note from the Author

As you may wish to read other versions of some of these traditional stories, I would like to acknowledge some of the sources I have referred to, although most of these stories can be found in several collections.

'The Shepherd and the Clever Princess' from 'Timo and the Princess Vendla' and 'The Amazing Pine Cone' from 'The Two Pine Cones' in *Tales from a Finnish Tupa* by J. Lloyd Bowman and M. Blanco, A. Whitman & Co., Chicago. 'The Boastful Toad' from *Folk Lore and Fable*, The Harvard Classics, ed. Charles W. Eliot, P.F. Collier and Son Company, New York, 1909. 'The Kind Parrot' from *West African Folk Tales*, Jack Berry, Northwestern University Press, Evanston, Illinois, 1991. 'The Dog and the Wolf' from *Aesop*, or from *The Fables of La Fontaine*, Richard Scarry, Doubleday and Company Inc., Garden City, New York, 1963. 'The Mole's Bridegroom' from *Asian-Pacific Folktales and Legends*, ed. Jeannette Faurot, Touchstone, New York, 1995.